Anansi Goes Fishing

retold by Eric A. Kimmel

illustrated by Janet Stevens

Holiday House / New York

To Lindsey and Blake
E.A.K.

To Mom H. and all the gang
J.S.

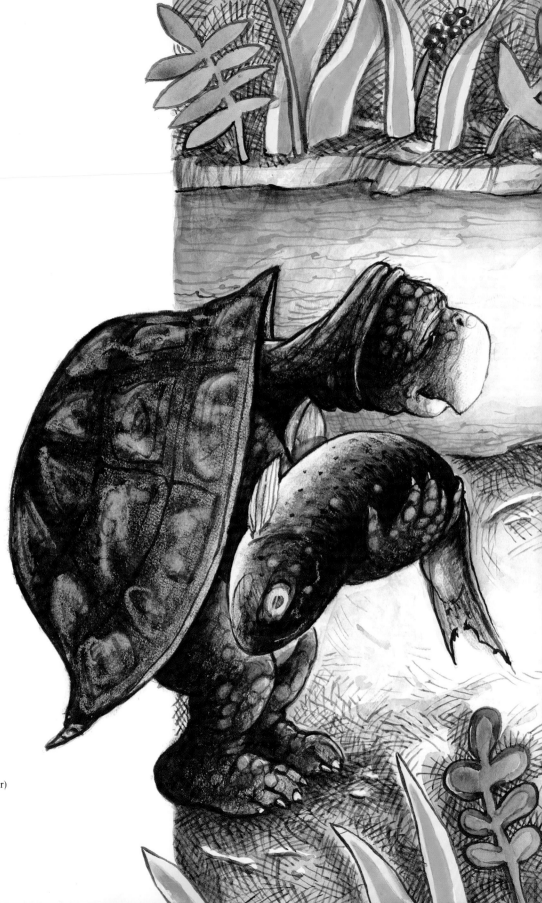

ISBN-13: 978-0-8234-0918-1 (hardcover)
ISBN-13: 978-0-8234-1022-4 (paperback)

Text copyright © 1992 by Eric A. Kimmel
Illustrations copyright © 1992 by Janet Stevens
Printed and bound in September 2013 at Tien Wah Press,
Johor Bahru, Johor, Malaysia.
All rights reserved
Library of Congress Cataloging-in-Publication Data

Kimmel, Eric A.
Anansi goes fishing / adapted
by Eric A. Kimmel ; illustrated by Janet Stevens. — 1st ed.
p.   cm.
Summary: Anansi the spider plans to trick Turtle into catching a
fish for his dinner, but Turtle proves to be smarter and ends up
with a free meal. Explains the origin of spider webs.
13 15 17 19 20 18 16 14 12
1. Anansi (Legendary character)   [1. Anansi (Legendary character)
2. Folklore—Africa. 3. Spiders—Folklore.] I. Stevens, Janet,
ill. II. Title.
PZ8.1.K567Ap   1991   91-17813   CIP   AC
398.24′52544—dc20

HOLIDAY HOUSE is registered in the U.S. Patent and Trademark Office.

One fine afternoon Anansi the Spider was walking by the river when he saw his friend Turtle coming toward him carrying a large fish. Anansi loved to eat fish, though he was much too lazy to catch them himself. "Where did you get that fish?" he asked Turtle.

"I caught it today when I went fishing," Turtle replied.

"I want to learn to catch fish too," Anansi said. "Will you teach me?"

"Certainly!" said Turtle. "Meet me by the river tomorrow. We will go fishing together. Two can do twice the work of one."

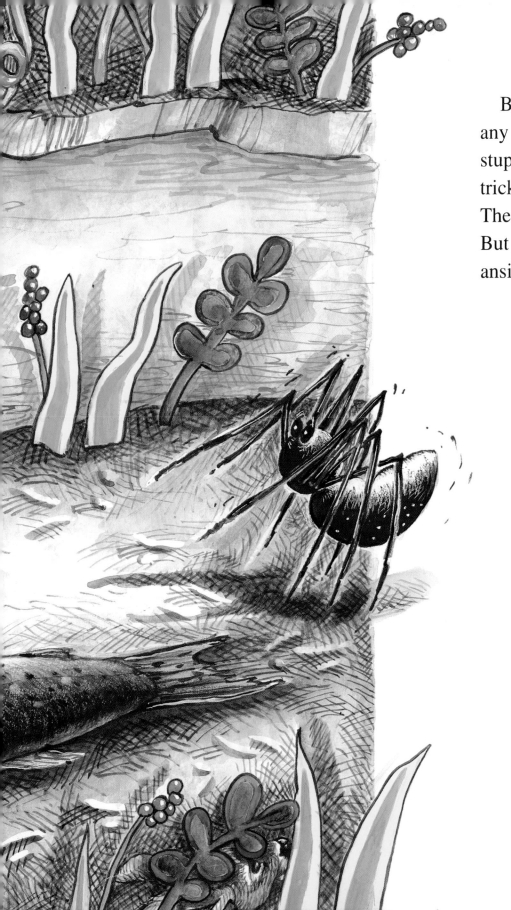

But Anansi did not intend to do any work at all. "Turtle is slow and stupid," he said to himself. "I will trick him into doing all the work. Then I will take the fish for myself." But Turtle was not as stupid as Anansi thought.

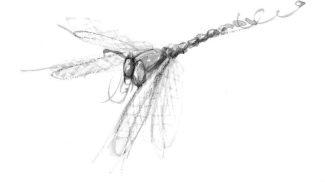

Early the next morning, Turtle arrived. "Are you ready to get started, Anansi?" he asked.

"Yes!" Anansi said. "I have been waiting a long time. I want to learn to catch fish as well as you do."

"First we make a net," said Turtle. "Netmaking is hard work. When I do it myself, I work and get tired. But since there are two of us, we can share the task. One of us can work while the other gets tired."

"I don't want to get tired," Anansi said. "I'll make the net. You can get tired."

"All right," said Turtle. He showed Anansi how to weave a net. Then he lay down on the riverbank.

"This is hard work," Anansi said.

"I know," said Turtle, yawning. "I'm getting very tired."

Anansi worked all day weaving the net. The harder he worked, the more tired Turtle grew. Turtle yawned and stretched, and finally he went to sleep. After many hours the net was done.

"Wake up, Turtle," Anansi said. "The net is finished."

Turtle rubbed his eyes. "This net is strong and light. You are a fine netmaker, Anansi. I know you worked hard because I am very tired. I am so tired, I have to go home and sleep. Meet me here tomorrow. We will catch fish then."

The next morning Turtle met Anansi by the river again.
"Today we are going to set the net in the river," Turtle said.

"That is hard work. Yesterday you worked while I got tired, so today I'll work while you get tired."

"No, no!" said Anansi. "I would rather work than get tired."

"All right," said Turtle. So while Anansi worked hard all day setting the net in the river, Turtle lay on the riverbank, getting so tired he finally fell asleep.

"Wake up, Turtle," Anansi said, hours later. "The net is set. I'm ready to start catching fish."

Turtle yawned. "I'm too tired to do any more today, Anansi. Meet me here tomorrow morning. We'll catch fish then."

Turtle met Anansi on the river-bank the next morning.

"I can hardly wait to catch fish," Anansi said.

"That's good," Turtle replied. "Catching fish is hard work. You worked hard these past two days, Anansi. I think I should work today and let you get tired."

"Oh no!" said Anansi. "I want to catch fish. I don't want to get tired."

"All right," said Turtle. "Whatever you wish."

Anansi worked hard all day pulling the net out of the river while Turtle lay back, getting very, very tired.

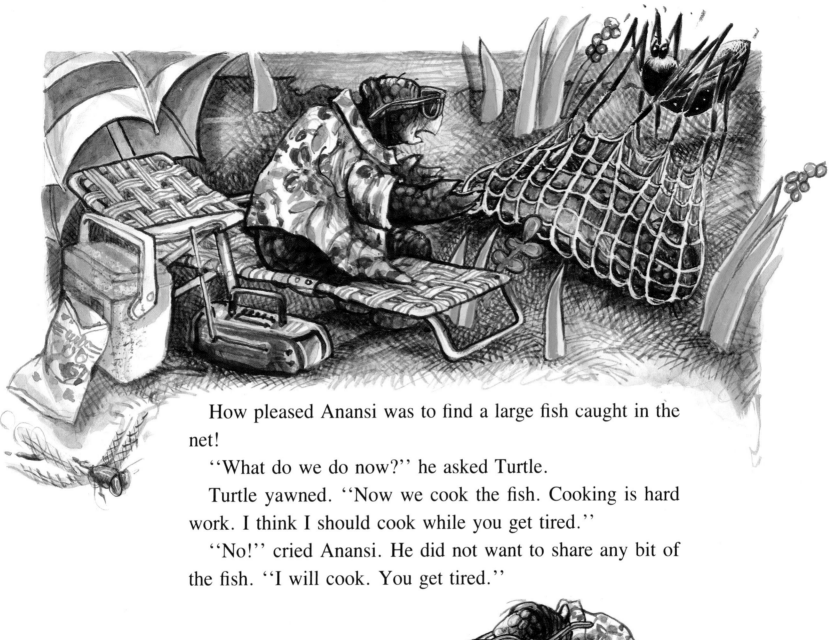

How pleased Anansi was to find a large fish caught in the net!

"What do we do now?" he asked Turtle.

Turtle yawned. "Now we cook the fish. Cooking is hard work. I think I should cook while you get tired."

"No!" cried Anansi. He did not want to share any bit of the fish. "I will cook. You get tired."

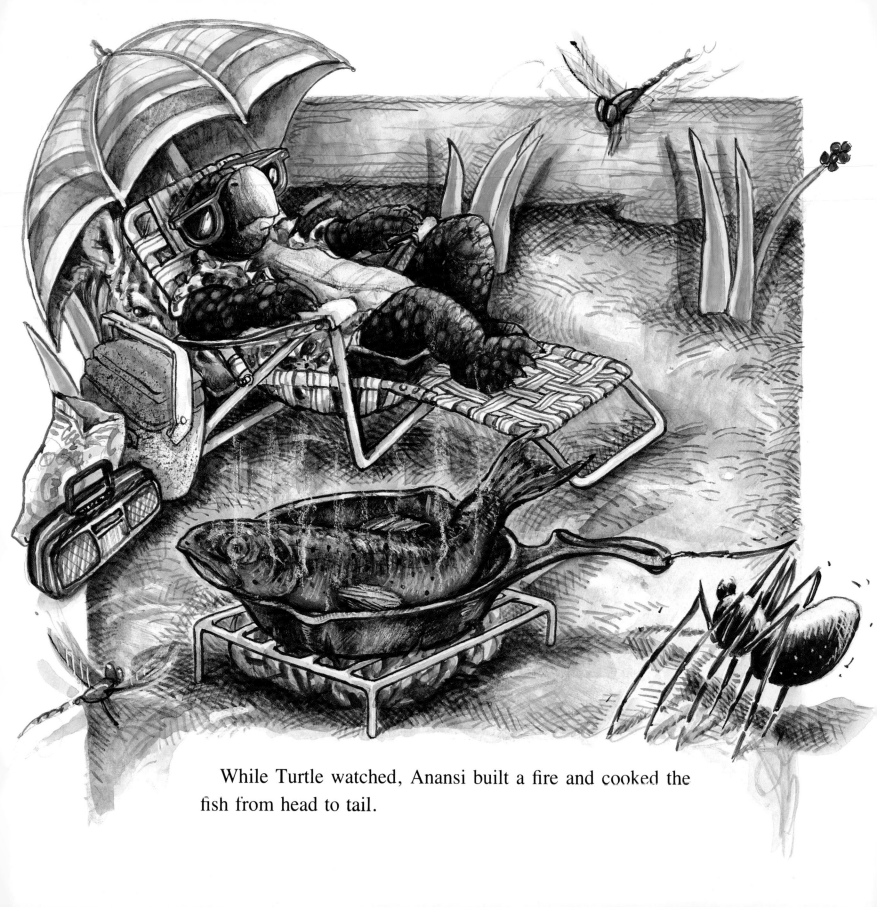

While Turtle watched, Anansi built a fire and cooked the fish from head to tail.

"That fish smells delicious," Turtle said. "You are a good cook, Anansi. And you worked hard. I know, because I am very, very tired. Now it is time to eat the fish. When I eat by myself, I eat and get full. Since there are two of us, we should share the task. One of us should eat while the other gets full. Which do you want to do?"

"I want to get full!" Anansi said, thinking only of his stomach.

"Then I will eat." Turtle began to eat while Anansi lay
back and waited for his stomach to get full.

"Are you full yet?" Turtle asked Anansi.
"Not yet. Keep eating."

Turtle ate some more. "Are you full yet?"
"No. Keep eating."

Turtle ate some more. "Are you full yet?"
"Not at all," Anansi said. "I'm as empty as when you started."

"That's too bad," Turtle told him. "Because I'm full, and all the fish is gone."

"What?" Anansi cried. It was true. Turtle had eaten the whole fish. "You cheated me!" Anansi yelled when he realized what had happened.

"I did not!" Turtle replied.

"You did! You made me do all the work, then you ate the fish yourself. You won't get away with this. I am going to the Justice Tree."

Anansi ran to the Justice Tree. Warthog sat beneath its branches. Warthog was a fair and honest judge. All the animals brought their quarrels to him.

"What do you want, Anansi?" Warthog asked.

"I want justice," Anansi said. "Turtle cheated me. We went fishing together. He tricked me into doing all the work, then he ate the fish himself. Turtle deserves to be punished."

Warthog knew how lazy Anansi was. He couldn't imagine him working hard at anything. "Did you really do all the work?" he asked.

"Yes," Anansi replied.

"What did you do?"

"I wove the net.

I set it in the river.

I caught the fish,

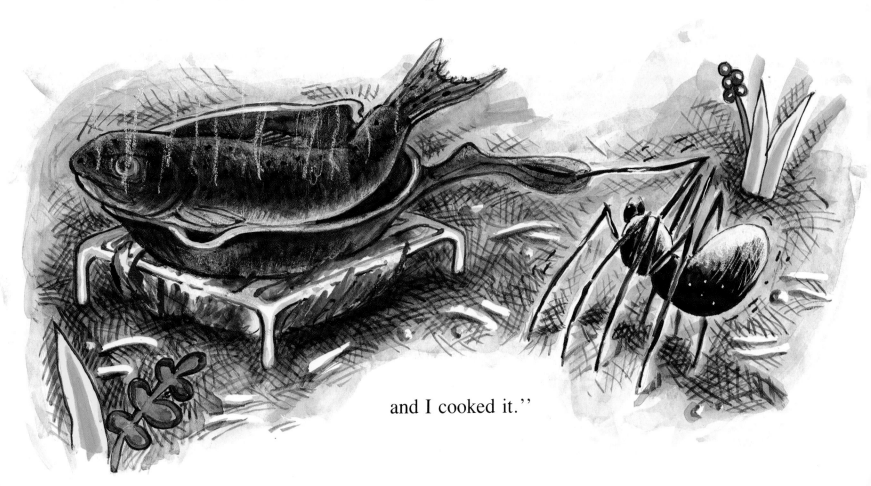

and I cooked it.''

"That is a lot of work. You must have gotten very tired."

"No," said Anansi. "I didn't get tired at all. Turtle got tired, not me."

Warthog frowned. "Turtle got tired? What did he do?"

"Nothing!"

"If he did nothing, why did he get tired? Anansi, I don't believe you. No one gets tired by doing nothing. If Turtle got tired, then he must have done all the work. You are not telling the truth. Go home now and stop making trouble."

Warthog had spoken. There was nothing more to be said. Anansi went home in disgrace, and it was a long time before he spoke to Turtle again.

But some good came out of it. Anansi learned how to weave nets and how to use them to catch food. He taught his friends how to do it, and they taught their friends. Soon spiders all over the world were weaving. To this day, wherever you find spiders, you will find their nets.

They are called ''spider webs.''